Elliot's
NOISY NIGHT

To Rachel and Mira

Elliot Moose™ Andrea Beck Inc.
Text and illustrations © 2002 Andrea Beck Inc.

Kids Can Press acknowledges the financial support of the Ontario Arts Council, the Canada Council for the Arts and the Government of Canada, through the BPIDP, for our publishing activity.

Published in Canada by
Kids Can Press Ltd.
29 Birch Avenue
Toronto, ON M4V 1E2

Published in the U.S. by
Kids Can Press Ltd.
2250 Military Road
Tonawanda, NY 14150

www.kidscanpress.com

The artwork in this book was rendered in pencil crayon. The text is set in Minion.

Edited by Debbie Rogosin
Designed by Karen Powers
Printed and bound in Hong Kong, China, by Book Art Inc., Toronto
This book is smyth sewn casebound.

CM 02 0 9 8 7 6 5 4 3 2 1

National Library of Canada Cataloguing in Publication Data

Beck, Andrea, 1956–
    Elliot's noisy night

"An Elliot Moose story."

ISBN 1-55337-011-2

I. Title.

PS8553.E2948E465 2002   jC813'.54   C2002-900064-5
PZ7.B380767Eln 2002

Kids Can Press is a /o∩us™ Entertainment company

Elliot's
NOISY NIGHT

Written and Illustrated by
ANDREA BECK

KIDS CAN PRESS

ELLIOT MOOSE was worried.

Last night, he'd heard noises in bed.

And though he'd managed not to think about them much all day, now that it was dark he couldn't think of anything else.

As he hurried to the kitchen for a bedtime snack, Elliot imagined scary things.

"Did anyone hear noises last night?"
Elliot asked his friends.

"Noises?" replied Socks.

"Yes, bumping and whooshing," said Elliot.
"It sounded like something was in the house.
I hid under my covers all night!"

"Bumping?" said Paisley.

"Whooshing?" whimpered Puff.

Everyone moved closer together.

But when Amy arrived with cookies
still warm from the oven, Elliot's
friends became quite brave.

"It must have been a dream," said Socks.

"Or your imagination," said Amy.

"I think it was an Elliot-eating monster!" hooted Angel.

And everyone laughed, even Elliot.

Elliot's friends chattered on, but he kept thinking about the noises.

What if there *was* something in the house?

The closer it got to bedtime, the more frightened he became. He wanted to tell Socks or Paisley. But what if everyone laughed again?

Elliot decided to go see Beaverton instead.

Elliot was almost at Beaverton's cupboard when he heard a noise.

WHIR-WHIR-WHUMP!

He burst through Beaverton's door and slammed it shut behind him.

"There's something out there!" he cried. "Listen!"

But as they put their ears to the door, Elliot noticed that Beaverton didn't seem worried. After listening very carefully, Elliot grinned.

"It's the fridge!" he exclaimed.

Beaverton grinned, too.

"I knew you'd figure it out," he said.

As Beaverton walked
Elliot to bed, they talked
about the other noises
Elliot had heard.

"No wonder you've got
the willies!" said Beaverton.
"Don't worry Elliot, house
noises sound louder at night. The furnace whooshes.
The floors creak. The shutters bang in the wind. Lionel
and I are so used to it, we never wake up anymore."

Elliot felt better. But he brought Beaverton's
flashlight to bed, just in case.

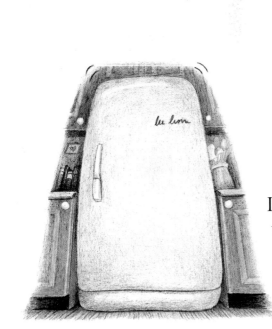

Later, Elliot awoke with a start.
WHIR-WHIR-WHUMP!
came a noise.
He shivered. Then he
remembered the fridge.
WHOOOOOOSHHHH!
He quivered. Then he remembered the furnace.
BUMP! BUMP! BANG!
Elliot closed his eyes and smiled. He wasn't going to
be frightened by a silly loose shutter.
But then Elliot heard something else.

SHUFFLE. SHUFFLE. SHUFFLE.

Elliot's tummy jumped.

Beaverton hadn't explained shuffling sounds.

What could they be?

Suddenly, a ghostly figure appeared in his doorway, and Elliot's fur stood right up on end!

"Are you awake?" came a wavering voice.

Elliot shrank deep beneath his covers.

But as the figure came closer, Elliot noticed pajamas and a pink blanket. It was Socks! Her slippers were making the shuffling sound.

"I heard bumping," whispered Socks.

"Don't worry," said Elliot bravely. "It's just the wind blowing the shutters."

Socks wanted to sleep over, just in case. So they snuggled down together in Elliot's cozy bed.

A moment later, the friends heard a loud THUMP!

It wasn't the fridge or the furnace. And it didn't sound like the shutters either.

Elliot and Socks grabbed each other's paws.

THUMP, THUMP!

They dove under the covers.

THUMP, THUMP!

Suddenly, the covers were snatched away!

"Something's following us!" cried Amy and Paisley. And they jumped into Elliot's bed.

THUMP, THUMP! came the noise again.

"Something's coming!" cried Snowy and Puff. And they jumped into Elliot's bed, too.

THUMPETY, THUMP, THUMP!

Angel came barreling out of the darkness.

"I hear noises!" she shrieked.

And she leapt into Elliot's bed.

All of a sudden, the thumping stopped. The friends listened, wide-eyed.

After a minute Amy sighed. "*We* made those thumping noises!" she cried.

Everyone groaned. Then they giggled. Then they settled down for the night.

One by one the friends fell asleep, except for Elliot, who felt rather crowded. So only Elliot heard the scariest sound of all.

SWISHHHH, SWISHHHH!

He froze.

What could it be?

Lionel? Beaverton?

No. They never woke up at night. And all of Elliot's other friends were in his bed.

SWISHHHH, SWISHHHH!

Maybe there was an Elliot-eating monster after all!

The sound came closer and closer.
Elliot's tummy scrunched into a knot.
What should he do?

He fumbled for Beaverton's flashlight.
Slowly, carefully, he brought it up from
under the covers. Then, trembling from head
to toe, Elliot waited.

When the swishing came right to his
door, he took a deep breath and turned on
the flashlight.

CLICK!

"OH!" gasped Beaverton.

"Beaverton?" whispered Elliot.

"This noisy night even woke *me* up!" said Beaverton. "I thought I should check on you." Then he noticed the others. "A sleepover. Oh boy!"

Beaverton hurried off to get his blanket and pillow, his tail swish-swishing behind him. Then he snuggled down, too.

It was the biggest sleepover ever!

Elliot smiled. Then he turned off the flashlight.
Click.
And at last, he fell asleep — safe and warm in
his noisy old house.

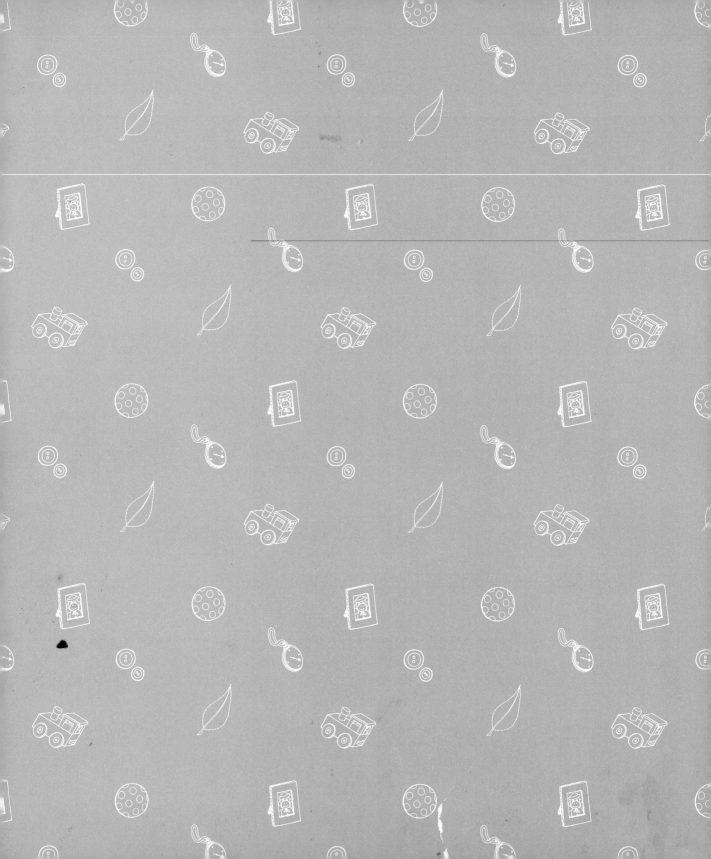